MW01056575

This book belongs to

_____

There's a Spider in My Bathtub
The Hug A Bug Tales Series
Copyright © 2021 April Eckert
Editor: Rob Daniel
Cover design and page layout: Catherine Knorr

Library of Congress Control Number: 2021905728

ISBN 978-1-7368648-1-4

Hug A Bug Publishing LLC
www.aprileckert.com

For my Millie,
I hope to inspire you to love ALL the
things, especially the smallest and
most misunderstood.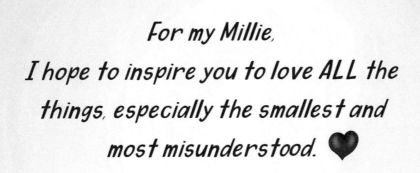

There's a spider in my bathtub
And I don't know what to do
If I run to get my mom
It might crawl someplace new.

It could end up on the toilet
Or even in the sink
I should run some water
And rinse it down, I think.

2

But if I rinse that spider
Who knows where it would go

A beach
a boat
a farm
a float

3

A **DINOSAUR**'s big toe?

4

Riding on that dino's toe
That's so big and hairy
Makes our little spider friend
Grow super scared and wary.

5

And if that silly dino
Finds our little friend
He'll raise his tiny arms
And kick him to Earth's end.

6

Flying out from Earth's green land
Little spider looks left and right

He finds a comfy meteor
From which to enjoy the flight.

But our little spider
Doesn't rest too long
Up ahead he sees lots of rocks
And things seem **very** wrong.

8

The rock he's on zings and zips

The spider cannot hold

He grasps that rock with all eight legs
But ends up getting rolled.

Stars and space all around
Our spider goes afloat

As he falls back to ground
He spies a castle moat.

He hurtles down towards the land
Faster and faster he flies

Until he hits a dragon's head
Right between the eyes.

(14)

That dragon goes down without a fight
And spider flies on back

15

He lands atop a knight's sharp sword
And readies for an attack.

16

But instead of hurting our furry friend
The knight just bows in awe
And says out loud, to the spider's surprise
"I'm *stunned* by what I just saw."

"You my brave little spider
Have saved my life today

For this, you will be knighted
Before going on your way."

18

And then the knight

brought down his shield

and revealed...

19

a *female's* face!

Her long brown locks cascaded down
She said, "Welcome to Fairview Place!"

20

"I am Queen Millie Irene.
Thank you for saving me.
I will bestow the knighthood
upon you.
Please get down on
one knee."

The Queen then asked for the spider's name
But he had none that he knew
So the Queen exclaimed,
"**Sir Simon** will do.
I knight you, Sir Simon of Fairview."

22

As the spider kneeled and closed his eyes
I shook my head with wonder.

Who knew this spider was
a knight
He deserves **more** than my near
blunder.

There's a spider in my bathtub
And I **now** know what to do
I will let this spider go
So he can start anew.

25

Out the window I set him down
And send him on his way

"Go on, Sir Simon the Spider
Make the **MOST** of your brand new day!"

26

Hi friends!
Sir Simon the Spider here!
I hope you enjoyed the adventure as much as I did!
I am very happy to finally be free. Honestly, I wish I
could have stayed in the house, but I'm thankful to have
a chance to have another exciting adventure! If you
enjoyed this story please take a minute to leave a review
on Amazon. I know the author would be very thankful.
See you in the next book!

P.S. Did you see my friend, duck?? He can be a bit sneaky
and he loves to hang around in the weirdest places, but
he was on almost every page! I hope you had fun spotting
him throughout the story!

Meet the Author!

As a child, April Eckert loved the outdoors. She could usually be found making mud pies and tree leaf soup, along with playing with worms and slugs in her spare time. Although nature was her favorite place, the one part of it that she was never comfortable with, was spiders.

As an adult, April has earned her Master's degree in Education. She has been a teacher for over 10 years and continues her love for nature. April is happiest playing outside amongst the trees, with her daughter.

Although spiders still aren't her favorite of the cute crawlies, she has learned that her childhood fear was based on not understanding these eight-legged creatures. She hopes that her books help children find their love for all things nature and their parents to be able to reconnect to the care-free feeling that being outside used to bring.

Meet the Illustrator!

Catherine fell in love with art at age 10, because of all the amazing worlds she visited when she read books. She would stare at the pictures, savoring every detail. That never changed, even as she grew up, got married, and had children.

Now, most days you'll see her with a cup of coffee in one hand and an ink smudge on the other. She rarely leaves home without her sketchbook, ready to capture a beautiful thought at any moment.

www.artbycatherineknorr.com

Four Reasons Why Spiders Are Our Friends

1 Spiders help keep the house free of insects like mosquitos, roaches, and fleas.

2 Spiders are not aggressive. They bite in self-defense, but most aren't strong enough to actually puncture the skin. Even if a spider bites and breaks the skin, most spiders are not poisonous to humans.

3 Our gardens are kept safe from harmful insects thanks to spiders keeping their populations in check!

4 Scientists are researching certain spider venom as a way to stop pain in humans.

Made in the USA
Las Vegas, NV
09 March 2024